ONE GOOD TURN

Chris Ryan

BBC
LARGE
PRINT

First published in 2008 by
Arrow Books
This Large Print edition published
2008 by BBC Audiobooks by
arrangement with
The Random House Group

ISBN 978 1 405 62233 2

British Library Cataloguing in Publication Data available

Printed and bound in Great Britain by
CPI Antony Rowe, Chippenham, Wiltshire

CHAPTER ONE

The man hurt in his dream and he hurt when he woke.

He was lying on a metal bed frame in a dark cellar. He was cuffed to it by the wrists and ankles. High up towards the ceiling, a cracked airbrick let in a little light so that he could see the bare walls, piles of rotting furniture and a wine rack along the far wall. The floor was puddled with water and the man could hear things running around in it.

Something moved at the bottom of the bed. Before he could react, a weight moved up his leg and onto his chest. He lifted his head and saw a big, greasy rat squatting on him. He bellowed and threw himself from side to side. The rat flopped off onto the wet floor.

He didn't go to sleep again. His

head was splitting. The rats were everywhere and behind their grunting and scratching he could always hear the guns.

Crump. Crump. Crumpcrump-crumpumpmpmpmpumpcrump. Crump. Crump.

That sound came from the big French guns down the line. You didn't just hear them. You felt them loosely in the gut.

The war taught you to recognise the different guns.

Eighteen-pound field guns went whizzzzz-BANG, depending on how close they were to the target. Once you heard the whizz, there wasn't much time till the bang. The German field guns sounded the same.

Mortars, which lobbed bombs high in the air to land on an enemy's head, made three distinct noises. POUM as the round was launched, EEEEEE as it flew through the air and CRACK as it landed.

The big shells, the Pissing Jennies

or Whistling Percies, screamed, then cracked the heavens open when they burst. They came from the heavy artillery as far as six miles behind the lines. A big gun might fire a sixty-pound shell but they were tiddlers compared to the big howitzers. These massive weapons slid along on special railways and fired 700-pound rounds.

His personal nightmare was the enemy's M11 mortar—a huge brute that fired an 850-pound shell, practically the weight of a horse. The M11 could blow a hole through four feet of reinforced concrete, or make a crater twenty-five feet deep. When you heard one of those screaming overhead, you knew men were going to die. Because the British Army thought concrete protection was cowardly and, anyway, you couldn't dig more than eight foot down into the Belgian mud without drowning.

The sound of one shell bursting was bad. Two was enough to bring tears to your eyes. Bombardments could often last for hours—days even—with the shells bursting every few seconds.

It was odd that he knew these things but did not know who he was. It was odd that the bed had no mattress and he was lying on its metal base. And it was odd that he was cuffed at the head and the feet so he could not move. In fact, everything was odd.

He heard a scraping sound and turned his head.

Christ, that hurt. His skin felt as if it had been scoured with sand and then dried until it cracked. His head was splitting. His jaw was loose. His tongue felt rough stumps where teeth should be. The entire length of his back felt raw. And the rawness went all the way down the backs of his legs. A distance away and above him, light flared as the cellar door opened.

A figure appeared, a dark shape

against the light, and footsteps sounded on creaky wooden stairs.

'Mate. Mate,' he called out hoarsely. 'What's going on, mate?'

The voice was cold and cruel. 'Don't "mate" me you horrid little man.' A face loomed over him, twisted with hate. 'You're lucky you weren't shot on the spot.'

The man watched as the figure turned, pulled a bottle of wine from a rack and left. The man on the bed started to cry. That was odd too. He cried himself back to sleep.

*   *   *

He dreamed he was up to his neck in filthy water in a shell hole with sides of slippery clay. He was holding onto what he thought were tree roots, but when he looked again, he saw they were human limbs. The thirst was torturing him, but he couldn't drink because the water was a stew of rotting flesh and mud. He felt movement near him in the water and a body bumped up against him, swollen by the gas of rot.

He held his breath and sank down. Immediately he was lost in a chaos of twisting guts and grasping hands. They felt round his neck. They felt in his pockets. He tried to kick himself free, but every time his face broke the surface he was dragged down into filth. He opened his mouth to shout but a hand clasped his mouth. Tighter. Tighter. Tighter.

He woke up to find a lantern shining in his face, a hand over his mouth and a rough voice telling him to shut up. The ties were taken off his wrists, and he was made to sit up.

'What's going on?' he whispered. He was so thirsty he could hardly speak.

'Scrubbing you up, mate.' An impossibly clean sergeant stood by the bed. Behind was a corporal with his Lee Enfield rifle at the ready.

'I'm thirsty.'

'All in good time. Here. Wash your face, then wash your hands,' the sergeant said.

'Tell me what's going on. Please.'

'You're a prisoner—that's what's going on. Now get a move on.'

A bowl of soap-scummed water was put in his lap but, instead of washing, the man dipped his face into it and drank. It was beautiful— the best thing he had ever drunk in his life. Only then did he splash it on his face. As the water grew steadily more filthy, he felt as if were washing away some of the horror.

'Now, you're a pretty boy again, we'll take you upstairs,' the sergeant said. 'My advice is to say as little as possible. It'll only piss them off.'

But when the man tried to stand he fell over. So he was supported by two privates up the stairs, down a dark corridor and into a long, cold room which was so full of light it hurt him. Through his tears, he saw three men sitting at a table at the end of the room, and felt himself being carried towards it.

'Why are you holding him up, Sergeant?' a voice snapped.

'He's prone to falling over, sir.'

'Nonsense. This is a field court martial, not a bloody rest home. He's a little coward with no spine. Let go of him, and if he falls, stamp on his hand or foot or something until he stands on his own. Christ and all the angels, he stinks! Let's get this over and done with.'

The sergeant put a chair in front of him. He leaned his weight on the back of it, and stared at the three officers who sat behind the long trestle table straight ahead. From their expressions, they didn't much like him. The lieutenant on the left had slicked-back fair hair, a thin moustache and looked younger than him, but then you could never tell with officers. The officer in the middle, a major, was balding and red-faced with heavy jowls. The officer on the right, another lieutenant, had a centre parting, a monocle and looked appalled.

The man did not grasp anything that followed. It concerned a man called John Stubbs and he didn't see why that should bother him.

'Right,' the major said. 'Let's get this going. Which of you is going to be the prisoner's friend? Hmm. Lieutenant Burton—I'm appointing you. Has the prisoner had time to prepare his defence?'

Lieutenant Burton, the one with the monocle, said: 'When was he arrested, Sergeant Major?'

'Two days ago, sir.'

'Plenty of time then,' the major said. 'Prisoner, I'm the president of this court martial. Lieutenant Burton is referred to as the Prisoner's Friend, which means he's defending you. Lieutenant Carpenter here is prosecuting. Is that clear? Good. As the president of the court, I run things. Now, I'm going to read out a

9

list of charges and then you tell us whether you want to plead guilty or not guilty. Is that clear? Good. Right.'

He looked down at a piece of paper on the tablecloth in front of him and read from it. 'Your name is Private John Stubbs of the London Battalion, Royal Fusiliers, 58th Division, etc, etc. The charges as they stand are that on the 23rd of September in this year of Our Lord nineteen hundred and seventeen, you did wilfully attempt to injure yourself to avoid discharging your duty as a soldier. At some point later in the day, you did steal from a fellow soldier leave papers and identification in order to impersonate same soldier. In other words you are a thief and a coward. How do you plead?'

The man was aware that all the officers were staring at him. He smiled at them vaguely.

'The man's an idiot,' the major

said. 'Lieutenant Burton, will you enter a plea, as the prisoner's friend?'

'Guilty,' the lieutenant said.

'Very well.' His pen scratched slowly across the paper. 'Um, Lieutenant Carpenter, can you take the court through what happened in greater detail, as it will have some bearing on the sentence? And for God's sake talk slowly and keep it brief because I've got to write it all down.'

The officer started talking about the war, but the prisoner was not interested in that any more. He was staring at the view outside the high windows. Heavy rain in northern Europe had made the summer of 1917 one of the wettest on record, but today the sun was out. The flowers in the overgrown beds glowed brightly. Rooks circled the crown of a huge chestnut tree. Beyond the garden, a wheat field was turning gold. Next to the wheat was a green meadow where a brown cow with gentle eyes rubbed its neck on a gate. And above it all, white clouds drifted peacefully across a pale blue sky.

To the prisoner, the view outside the window was like medicine. For almost a year, he had been frightened of the sky because of all the awful things that fell out of it: shells, poison gas, or more of the dreadful, smothering rain.

The only bright colours he had seen had been the acid white of flares, the dirty yellow of shell bursts, the crimson brightness of blood and the purple of spilled guts. The only trees he had seen were blasted stumps. The only fields he had walked on had been turned into a sucking, poisonous soup of brown mud by years of bombing. The only harvest from these fields were the bodies of his comrades and enemies, mown down by machine guns, buried by mud, blown up by shells, buried again, blown up again.

The sergeant was bellowing in his ear.

'Have you got anything to say, Private? Answer the court!'

'I'm so sorry,' the man answered. 'About what?'

'This is the clearest case of contempt I have ever seen,' the major said. 'I've never seen the like. At present we have no findings to announce. We will be taking evidence with regard to the prisoner's character. But in my opinion, Private Stubbs, you are a thief, a coward and quite possibly a murderer. Unless defence has anything to add, I now pronounce the proceedings in open court to be over.'

It was only as he was being marched out that the penny dropped. He was John Stubbs. That seemed to be the gist of it. And if he were John Stubbs, then he had done all those terrible deeds.

What strength he had left his legs again and he collapsed.

'Pick him up, lads and get him out,' the sergeant said. The prisoner was lifted up again by the two privates and they began to drag him out of the room. At the door he managed to turn his head.

'Wait,' he said. 'Wait! There's been a mistake! I'm not John Stubbs!'

He expected the world to stop but the three officers who had been seated at the table ignored him. The prosecutor and the court president were talking and the other, his defender, had got up. Now he was standing at the window, whacking his riding boots with a crop. He stopped, put his monocle back into his eye and looked at the prisoner.

'Are you saying we've been wasting our time?'

'Yes! No. I don't know.'

'What are you saying then?'

'Just that you've got the wrong man.'

'Who on earth are you then?' the officer asked.

The prisoner shook his head. 'I can't remember.'

The officer laughed like a horse. 'Well, you'd better try. Because if you're not John Stubbs, I don't know who is.'

CHAPTER TWO

John Stubbs saw the Chinese sailor weaving his way down Tooley Street and smiled to himself. Funny the things that you saw these days: women making bombs in factories all day, and drunk Chinamen in the middle of London on a Saturday morning when all God-fearing men and women should be serving King and Country—or taking it easy.

Not that anyone seemed to take it easy in the Great Port of London. For mile upon mile, the riverbanks were lined with great cranes and towering warehouses, deep docks and busy wharfs. From Tower Bridge to Greenwich, from Wapping to the Isle of Dogs, the Port of London was a vast throat that swallowed everything that came its way: food, timber, cloth, coal, iron—anything that the capital of the British Empire needed. And now the Empire was at war, and had been for two years, it was incredible what passed through the Port of London. And what opportunities there were for natural crooks like John Stubbs, native of Whitechapel, prize conman and thief.

Stubbs looked up and down the street. It was early and not yet busy. A potboy was sweeping the sawdust out of a pub down the road. A market trader had just come from Borough Market, his two-handed cart piled high with cabbages. Two clerks, neatly dressed in suits and bowler hats, walked into Hay's

Wharf, where, they said, all the tea in China was stored.

Stubbs wondered why they weren't in the army. Whatever the papers said, the war in France was going badly. When it had started two years ago, the papers had boasted that one knockout blow would stop the Hun in his tracks. The second blow would send him reeling back out of Belgium, back out of France, all the way to Germany.

As far as Stubbs could see, they had got it all wrong. The war wasn't like a boxing match fought according to the Queensberry Rules. This was a street fight with two punch-drunk idiots going at it in the mud: both too stubborn to give up, neither strong enough to win.

Sign up now, people had said. If you delay, the war will all be over and you'll miss the fun.

Men had signed up in their thousands, queuing in some places to make sure they were on a troopship to France and Belgium as soon as possible.

Where were they now?

Dead. Blown to bits by shells, hung up on barbed wire, cut in half by machine guns or drowned in the sodden trenches.

Stubbs knew this. He talked to the soldiers on leave as they spilled out of the stations at Waterloo and London Bridge, their pockets full of back pay, desperate for drink or a girl, or both. If the poor idiots met John Stubbs first, they'd find themselves drink-less, girl-less and money-less in double-quick time. He had more tricks up his sleeve than a conjuror and no one to please but himself.

The Chinese sailor was almost level with the doorway Stubbs was now leaning against. He stepped out in front of him and put a friendly hand on his shoulder

'Hello, chum,' he said. 'Been looking all over for you.'

The sailor looked at Stubbs drunkenly. Stubbs guessed he had been wandering around all night.

'You look for me? Why you look for me?' he said.

Stubbs winked. 'I told you I'd find you a girl and I have,' he whispered. 'She's young, she's beautiful, she's all yours and—' he pulled out a broken pocket watch and pretended to read it—'she's waiting. She's been waiting a long time for you and if you don't hurry, she'll go home, mate.'

The sailor looked confused. 'Girl for me?'

'Last night we had a drink. You said what you wanted and I said I'd help,' Stubbs said. 'I promised and I'm a man of honour. She is beautiful. So young. So . . .' He gestured with his hands and winked. 'You know what I mean. There's not much I can teach you.'

He pointed to a top-floor window in a small house crammed between two warehouses.

'She's up there!'

The window he was pointing at belonged to a small accountancy firm, but that didn't matter. The important thing was that its front door was hidden down an alleyway to the side of the building. Out of sight.

'You got money? Don't show me out here.' Stubbs winked again. He had seen the sailor's hand move to his purse. Now Stubbs knew it was on a string tied to his waistband, inside his trousers. 'Quick,' he said. 'Police coming. Quick!'

He pushed the sailor down the alley ahead of him. Then he whipped out his cosh and tapped the sailor on the back of his head, knocking him out. The purse was exactly where he thought it would be, and he cut it free with his clasp knife.

He walked away, tossing the purse in his hands: a bit of rent money, a bit of beer money and a bit of fun money. It was a good morning's work.

An angry shout from behind him made him stop and turn. A crowd of Chinese sailors had gathered around the mouth of the alleyway. Stubbs swore.

He should have made sure that the man was on his own. It looked like he had been part of a gang, and now half of China was on Stubbs's tail.

He started to run as fast as he could towards the brick tunnels under the station. On the other side lay a maze of narrow streets and yards that he knew like the back of his hand. He could hide out there all day, if he wanted, but he had to get there first! From the sound of the voices echoing down the tunnel behind him, they were gaining on him and he was getting tired. He'd had too much beer and too many fags.

Stubbs reached the end of the tunnel, skidded round the corner and ran straight into the biggest man he had ever seen. He bounced off him

21

and fell into the gutter, knocking his knee.

'WHOA THERE!'

Stubbs felt a large hand grab his collar, lift him in the air as if he were a child and put him down. The man was dressed in khaki, had three stripes on his arm and a large moustache.

'Let me go, let me go! They're after me!'

'All right, son. The army's here.'

'I can't move!' Stubbs shouted. 'You've crippled me, you great ox!'

'Crippled you, have I?' the giant said. 'We'll just have to see about that. Your luck is in because just across the road are some of the most skilled doctors in all the land. Let's just pop in there and get you sorted out, young man. Don't worry. We'll look after you.'

Stubbs felt himself pushed across the street and into a dark office where a man in khaki uniform was sitting at a low table.

He looked around. There were posters on the wall—YOUR COUNTRY NEEDS YOU.

'I'm not signing up,' Stubbs squeaked.

The huge sergeant stood back from the doorway he had been blocking. Outside, half a dozen Chinese sailors were standing in a group, pointing and shouting. A couple of them were waving long knives with wicked blades.

'Your choice, sonny,' he said. 'You can sign up or you can go out there and take your chances.'

'But they'll slice me up,' Stubbs said.

'They do seem rather angry. I'm afraid I don't speak their lingo so I can't reason with them. As I said, it's your choice: go out there or stay with us. Remember, the army looks after its own. If you volunteer, I'll see to it that you end up doing something that suits your particular skills. Let's see now. What would you think about a nice job in supplies? Maybe we could get you sorting out the rum ration. That's an important job. You might never even have to leave England. You might even stay here in London. What do you say, chum? A soft life for the next few years—or a Chinese knife in your guts?'

So Stubbs signed.

*   *   *

The first lesson Stubbs learned was that the army was as full of liars as Civvy Street—and the biggest liar of them all was the sergeant who had recruited him.

Three months training in a hellhole in the Welsh countryside taught him the ropes. He learned how to drill on a parade ground, shoot a rifle, bayonet a scarecrow. But most of all, he learned that that whatever people said about teamwork, in the army it was every man for himself.

He started a little boot- and buckle-shining business which went quite well until the military police found out about it and kicked the living daylights out of him. After that, he made sure they were cut in on all his scams—which grew to include the illegal sale of tobacco, whisky and pornographic postcards brought back from France.

All that came to an end when he was sent to war. He spent two days on a train, half a day on a boat and then another day on a train. If he'd paid any attention at all, he would have known that he was going to the Bullring: the huge training camp at Etaples where the recruits were knocked into shape by the Canaries—a staff of sadists and bullies.

John Stubbs got off the train and took stock. Even at six in the morning, the place was a sea of khaki. Men were being herded into lines ready to be marched off to the camp which was a mass of tents that stretched as far as the eye could see.

He sidled up to one of the guards who were there to stop the soldiers legging it down the railway lines.

'Busy day?' he asked.

The guard spat. 'Not really. Bit quiet actually.'

'Like this all the time, is it?'

'More or less.'

So, Stubbs thought, hundreds of men are arriving every hour. They've got to be going somewhere.

It didn't take a great deal of intelligence to work out where.

They were going to the front, where they were replacing the men who were being killed at the rate of hundreds an hour.

So Stubbs decided to stay put.

*   *   *

He quickly learned that the Bullring was in fact a series of training grounds. Each one was surrounded

26

by a city of sleeping tents, mess halls, kitchens, storehouses and depot tents. Each one used hand-painted road signs like those on the streets at home.

For the first week, Stubbs thought he would never find his way around. He was moved from one regiment to another, then back to his original one without anyone noticing that he had gone in the first place. No one cared. They just concentrated on making sure that within six weeks soldiers left the camp, ready to kill or be killed.

They did this by making the place as hellish as possible. Exercises took place with live ammunition and real hand grenades. After each exercise, stretcher-bearers took the injured away to the many field hospitals and casualty clearing stations that lay behind the lines.

By day ten at the Bullring, Stubbs had already seen one man put his bayonet through his best friend's thigh. Another blew his hand off while assembling a Mills bomb, one of the pineapple-shaped hand grenades that had just been developed.

He knew it was time to take action.

The only way to get out of the grinding, punishing routine was to go sick. People devised the most ingenious methods, such as stuffing their boots with blotting paper to make themselves faint on parade, or eating sour milk or old meat to mess up their guts. Some men even shot themselves, though this was dangerous. First, if the wound got infected, you might lose a limb or die. Secondly, if the military police suspected you had shot yourself, you would be court martialled for cowardice.

Stubbs knew that hundreds of thousands of tons of food, weapons, ammunition, clothing and machinery passed through the French countryside right under his nose.

Controlling the movement of all this stuff were the quartermasters, or Q Division. They were a section of the British Army whose job was to make sure the wheels of war kept rolling. Stubbs also knew that Q Division did not have access to medical supplies. And that was the chance he needed.

One morning he made sure he was first in line to see the medical orderly or MO. The MO sat behind a wooden trestle table, while a nurse stood at a table nearby, checking pills in a medicine cabinet.

Stubbs stood in front of the table and came straight to the point. 'I need some time to myself,' he said quietly. 'What's the best you can do for me?'

'I beg your pardon. What do you mean . . . ?'

Stubbs leaned across the table and, putting venom in his voice, he whispered: 'I know what you've got hidden at the bottom of your kitbag in your quarters, sir, and it's not postcards of the royal family.'

A few days ago he had been on cleaning duties in the officers' quarters and had taken the trouble to do some snooping. When he found the pictures of naked boys sunning themselves by the sea, he knew they would come in useful.

'That'll be all, nurse!' the doctor blurted out. He was a young man with serious eyes behind his round, horn-rimmed glasses.

'Sir?' the nurse said.

'Embarrassing problem with this one, nurse. Won't let me look at him with a lady in the room.'

'But sir, I've—'

'I know, I know, but just to make things move along.' As soon as she'd gone, he said: 'What do you mean?'

Stubbs smiled. 'I don't care if you like looking at pictures of little foreign boys sir, but I think I know what the brigadier calls it. Beastliness. Tut, tut. They shoot people for less.'

'But they're art!' the doctor said. 'They're beautiful!'

'They're illegal, sir. I know because I used to deal in them. Now, here's what I want.'

Two minutes later Stubbs had been bought off with the promise of a supply of morphine and a note, which said he had a broken rib and needed time off for it to heal.

Then he started work in earnest.

For two days, he waited. On the third he had got his man: a corporal working in the quartermasters' HQ. The corporal visited certain shops and officers' messes once in the morning on foot, and once in the afternoon with a supply wagon and a team of two horses.

He was taking orders in the morning and filling them in the afternoon, Stubbs thought. And from the way cash changed hands, he was sure that he was seeing stolen goods being sold through the black market.

On the fourth day, Stubbs waited for the wagon to slow down on a muddy slope and hopped onto it.

'Who the bloody hell are you?' the corporal said. He looked well fed and soft, to Stubbs. His yellow armband showed he was on the staff.

'I'm Private Desperate, that's who I am,' Stubbs said.

'Well, go and be desperate somewhere else,' the corporal replied, 'or you'll get a visit from my mates and then you really will be sorry.'

'I don't think so,' Stubbs said. 'Because I've got something you want.'

'What's that?'

'Morphine.'

'Why do you think I want morphine?' the man asked.

'Because this is hell,' Stubbs said. 'And people want out. Take morphine like the Chinese sailors take it, and you're wherever you want to be. I know you. I've been watching. Get me a soft bed, get me a yellow armband and you and me can really go places. I reckon morphine's the one thing you boys can't get hold of and, funnily enough, it's the one thing I can.'

When Stubbs was at school, there was one Latin phrase he learned between his frequent beatings: *carpe diem*. Seize the day, it meant. Or as his old grandmother used to say: nothing ventured, nothing gained.

Two days later, Stubbs was the personal servant of a Captain D'Arcy, whose full name was Lord Frederick Arthur D'Arcy. D'Arcy was hugely rich, as thick as a plank and a morphine addict. To be honest, Stubbs reckoned, the more drugs he took, the better it was for all concerned. God help the British Army if that joker ever got off his camp bed, and tried to do his bit for King and Country.

Stubbs's cushy job lasted two months. As long as his supply of morphine was there, he was left alone. But as soon as it dried up, it was all over. As demand for morphine increased, so the pressure on the doctor grew and in time he snapped. Instead of committing suicide, he gave up his job in the training camp and volunteered for the next best thing: to become attached to an infantry battalion on its way to the front for the next big push.

Without his supply of morphine, Stubbs's pet officer became very ratty. One day he woke up to find Stubbs going through his private letters, and it dawned on him that certain family heirlooms had gone missing recently. Now he came to think of it, this began when his new batman had arrived.

Captain D'Arcy was not a man to make a fuss, but he had gone to the right school and he knew the right people. That very day Stubbs was sent back to his old regiment. He was sent to the front with sixty pounds of kit on his back.

CHAPTER THREE

Now the prisoner's court martial was out of the way, he had been allowed to wash. He had found that the whole of his back was burned, as if he had been out in the fields for too long without a shirt. In two patches, the burning was more serious and his blisters covered raw flesh and pus.

A doctor had come in, taken a quick look at the weeping wounds and put a dressing on them. The prisoner knew why he hadn't taken more care: a firing squad was going to shoot him the morning after next. There was no point in wasting dressings on a man who was about to die, when there were men who could be saved elsewhere. Proper men. Proper heroes. Men who deserved to live.

The prisoner had also been unchained. He had moved an old chest, so that he could stand on it, underneath the broken airbrick. The light fell on his face and made him feel alive. And he liked trying to make out what the sounds were in the street outside: the rolling crunch of wagon wheels, the steady tramp of men marching, the murmur of French, the rare sound of birds.

Take two, do, take two. Take two, do, take two.

That was a woodpigeon.

Teacher, teacher, teacher.

That was a great tit.

All of a sudden he heard a voice in his head. 'And the yellowhammer, he goes: *a little bit of bread and no cheese.*'

That was his father.

A picture, as clear as day, appeared in his mind. His father was talking to him at the ford by the big gate onto the moor. He loved the ford when he was little, loved the way the brown, peaty water curled around the stones and washed away the mud of the sheep and cattle.

Dartmoor. That was it. He was from Dartmoor, and his father had a small farm on the edge of the moor outside the village of Lydford. They had a flock of sheep, a few cows and a couple of Dartmoor ponies because his mother loved them.

The memories lit up the prisoner's mind like a shaft of golden sunlight. They were almost too vivid to bear. He could see his mother making clotted cream to sell to the hotel down by the station; and himself, as a boy, dipping his fingers through the crust when she wasn't looking and letting the velvety taste melt on his tongue and slip down his throat. He remembered saddling up Mouse, his own pony which he had hand-reared, and riding out for long days on the moor, and he heard the curlews calling from the valleys and saw the rooks and the buzzards circling overhead.

He remembered the harsh winters, wading thigh-deep through the snow to feed the cattle and check on the sheep. He remembered taking the job in the squire's stables where he mucked out, and helped look after the two great hunters the squire kept. Castor and Pollux they were called, and there weren't two other horses like them in Devon.

He was sixteen when the war started. Everyone had a father, a brother, an uncle or a friend who was caught up in it. But when the army started recruiting in Tavistock, the nearest town, his mother wouldn't let him go. The squire said the same thing when he caught the boy moping behind the stables and asked what the matter was.

'Don't be such a bloody idiot,' he snapped. 'War is war and to be avoided at all costs. I lost my brother in South Africa. Know how he died?'

'A Zulu warrior?' the boy asked hopefully.

'No.'

'A Boer?'

'No. Nor was it the Queen of Sheba. It was dysentery. Do you know what he was doing? He was running a place called a concentration camp and the dysentery swept through it. And who was in the camp? Boer women and Boer children: held there so the army could burn their farms and shoot their animals. That's war,' the squire said. 'Only a fool wants to fight.'

'But I want to do my bit. I want to have a go at the Hun.'

'A few years ago the Hun was your brother,' the squire growled. 'Prince Albert, our own King's father, was a bloody Hun. The Queen was a bloody Hun. The bloody King's a bloody Hun, if you ask me.' He stormed off, hitting the nettles with his walking stick. 'They're all bloody

Huns!'

This had just left him even more miserable. How could he not fight when so many others of his age were joining the Devonshire Regiment? And what would it be like when they came home and found him still there, with straw in his hair and muck under his nails? The squire was bitter. That was all. For him it would be different.

*   *   *

He had left his sleeping parents with a loving goodbye note and had taken the 5.45 morning train from Lydford to Exeter. There he quickly found a recruiting station.

'How old are you, sonny?' the sergeant had asked.

'Seventeen, sir,' the prisoner had replied.

'Well, walk to the cathedral and back. By that time you'll be eighteen and old enough to enlist,' the

40

sergeant had said with a wink.

All went smoothly. Training camp in the north of England was not very pleasant, until the drill sergeant discovered that he had a way with horses. Then everything changed.

In the old days when you joined the army, it was said that you took the King's Shilling. It was a joke these days that a horse was worth more than a man, because a man might cost a shilling but a horse could cost anything up to £40. Every week, gypsy traders would drive their horses to the camp to sell them. The prisoner was standing by the ring one day while an officer was trying to choose a mount. He looked from the outside of the ring and eventually pointed to a lively bay with a blaze on its forehead.

The prisoner could not believe his eyes, so much so that he ran up to the officer and blurted out: 'You can't buy that!'

The horse trader looked daggers

at him. 'This is a fine horse,' he said. 'I've never seen the like and this gentleman is clever enough to spot it.'

'He's lame in the back leg. He's got no wind and his mouth's cut to ribbons, which means someone's tried to control him but failed. That's the best one in the ring,' he said, pointing to a quiet chestnut horse. 'He's strong and steady, but don't pay a penny over twenty quid for him.'

After that, he worked with horses and was happy.

*   *   *

Three weeks later he was in France, with the Artillery Brigade of the 7th Division.

The artillery couldn't work without horses. One of the horses' most important duties was to pull the field guns into position and keep them supplied with shells. As a good six-man gun crew could fire twenty rounds a minute for hours, the riders were kept busy bringing a supply of shells from the ammo dumps.

And it was true: the horses, wherever possible, were treated better than the men. They were stabled back from the lines, away from the worst of the German artillery fire; they did not live up to their knees in muddy water. And unlike a soldier, unless he was a high-ranking officer, each horse was looked after by a team of grooms and riders, who cared deeply for their animals.

The prisoner thought back to an event in July that summer, not so long ago. It was before the rains came, and the weather had been good. There had been rumours that the army was going to make a big push into Ypres, but no one took it seriously. He was experienced by then, but most of his work had been moving guns and ammunition behind the lines.

One morning, however, his sergeant, who was another Devon man called Sid Mitchell, had beckoned him over.

'Last night they moved four sections of B Battery forward,' Mitchell said grimly. 'They've been shot up badly and it's up to the lads of A Battery to keep them supplied.'

'What's the problem?' he asked. 'I mean, why is it worse than anything else?'

'Well, it's like this,' Sergeant Mitchell said. 'Our position is very exposed. All through the war, we've managed to keep hold of a sort of bulge that cuts into the enemy line. But here's the problem, son. This bulge is surrounded on three sides by enemy-held hills. That means our German chums can sit up there, bomb the hell out of us and we just have to take it. We've tried everything. We even dug under one of those hills and blew the whole

44

thing up with 91,000 pounds of high explosives. The Prime Minister heard the explosion in Downing Street but even that hasn't changed things. You still cannot move in that bulge without a German on a hill seeing you and shooting at you with a rifle, or a cannon, or a howitzer. They specially like shooting at artillery trains. Are you ready for it, mate?'

'As I'll ever be,' the prisoner said. He went to make sure his team of horses were ready, and that the ammunition wagon was tightly packed so the shells couldn't slip around.

*   *   *

He was riding his lead horse through bullets and shells and pieces of flying metal and pushing it as fast as he dared. The enemy guns knew exactly where they were, had their range and were waiting for them. As soon as they got onto the narrow road, the bombardment shattered the sky. Lumps of metal hissed past his head. High explosives churned up the marshy earth on either side of the road. The mud that showered them was mixed with fragments of corpses that lay there.

There was a scream from behind! He stopped. One of the horses in the team behind had lost half a leg. The beast was plunging and rearing, screaming with pain, and would soon drag the rest of the team and the ammunition wagon off the road and into the mud.

'Ride on,' Sergeant Mitchell shouted. 'Get out of here! Get this ammo forward and maybe our guns firing can keep them quiet for a while. It's our only chance!'

The boy got his team going again. Once they were moving, the horses were easier to control, if you could stop them bolting. He kept his eyes ahead, trying not to take in the scene beside the road: dead horses, dead men, bits of men. Ahead of him and to the sides, he could see the low hills where the Germans waited. The battery he was trying to reach was a quarter of a mile further on, where there was a drier patch of ground.

When he reached the field guns, they were silent. Two had been knocked out, and one was surrounded by shattered bodies. The only one with a fit crew had sunk so deep into the mud that its barrel was pointing at the sky.

He saw what he had to do.

He called one of the gunners over. 'Help me unhitch the ammo cart and we can pull your gun out of the mud with the horses!'

The gunners unhitched the wagon, and he led the frightened beasts across the mud to the gun. Men from the other guns saw what was going on and came to help, as enemy shells howled overhead and exploded in mid-air, showering them with shrapnel. He coaxed the horses forwards and managed to turn them so the traces could be hitched to the back of the gun.

'Come on, you beauty,' he whispered in the leading horse's ears. 'Get us out of here. Come on. COME ON!'

He swung himself onto the horse's back, and leaned over its head to urge it on. He saw the great sinews in its shoulder shiver, felt its feet slip, hold, slip, hold.

'COME ON!'

The hooves gripped. The wheel of the gun moved an inch, then two. The men put their shoulders against the spokes and pushed with new strength and forced the wheel from the grip of the mud.

The gun was free! The horses had done it.

One of the gunners came up to him. His face was grim but determined. 'We'll be able to work the gun now. Thanks. What's your name, mate?'

'Ransom,' he said. 'Private Chris Ransom.'

'Well, you deserve a bloody medal. Now get the hell out of here.' A drop of rain fell on his face. 'Great. Rain. That's all we bloody need.'

*   *   *

Back in his cellar, the prisoner breathed a sigh of relief. He had a name. Surely everything would be all right now.

CHAPTER FOUR

John Stubbs stood on the firing step of the trench, his gun snugly tucked into his shoulder. Above the trench, a rampart had been built out of sandbags—mudbags to be more accurate—and he was gazing through a tiny gap over no-man's land. Look through anything bigger and a sniper would put a bullet through your eye. Sometimes the men put an old steel helmet on a stick, held it above the rampart and took bets on how long it would be before it was shot. The shortest time Stubbs had seen was three seconds.

He saw a movement and fired. The rifle kicked back into his shoulder and immediately his hand moved to the bolt and fed another round into the breech. He fired again. The rat, horribly fat, was knocked backwards from its perch on the back of some poor sod who had died out there. Stubbs began to look for another one. It was better than doing nothing.

Rain ran off the brim of his tin helmet in a near solid waterfall. It fell on his front, his shoulders and down his back.

He was wet through, chilled to the bone and could not get any colder. In fact, he had been wet and cold for almost two months now, and had forgotten what it was like to be dry and warm. The big guns far behind their lines had started up before dawn. Shells moaned or whistled overhead, depending on their size. The ground shook.

The private next to him seemed to be shouting something. Even though he was only ten feet away, Stubbs couldn't hear a thing through the din. He pointed to his ear and shook his head.

The private glanced down the line, checking to make sure no one could see him leave his post, which was a court-martial offence, and shouted in Stubbs's ear: 'Attack's coming.'

Stubbs nodded.

'We're in the first wave.'

'Can't be,' Stubbs shouted back. 'We've been up here for eighteen hours. They always bring fresh troops up for an attack.'

'They've run out,' the private bawled back. 'Didn't you hear? The

Aussies got cut up something rotten in some wood or other. It's up to us to win the war, mate.' He spat and moved back to his post.

Stubbs had been in attacks before but never in the first wave and he had always managed to fall into a handy shell hole and act wounded. But a new, fire-eating captain had arrived who would not allow any of his men to shirk.

Stubbs hunched down and tried to think of a way out of this mess.

The Big Push had taken place at the end of July and, like every other big push, had failed. The plan was to advance out of the bulge at Ypres and take the German hills that surrounded it. The Germans would then have to move a few divisions down to the battle. This would take the pressure off the French and even encourage them to mount an attack. There had been rumours that the entire French army was on the point of mutiny.

In preparation, special miners had dug tunnels under Messines Ridge, filled them with explosives and blown the hill up in the biggest man-made explosion the world had ever seen. Twenty thousand Germans died in that single explosion. Over the following weeks, three thousand guns had fired four and a half million shells to cut the German wire and knock out their machine-gun posts.

Then the rains had started. And a good summer had turned into the wettest one on record. But the British Army never let details like that stop an advance. The only trouble was, when they tried to attack, they got stuck.

The ground, which was wet already, turned into something no one had ever seen before: a new substance somewhere between mud and water. If you fell off one of the duckboard roads, you drowned, even though there might be men marching alongside you, just a few feet away. If horses or mules fell into the mud, they had to be shot because they were too heavy to pull out, and there was no way they could ever struggle free.

To attack across such ground was impossible, but wave after wave of men were sent into battle, only to sink up to their waists in mud and get shot by the enemy. Others tried to take shelter in craters, where they drowned. (Just as a reminder that no one ever learns the lessons of war, a cemetery where Belgian and French soldiers had been buried during the first weeks of the war, was blown up. The bodies were blown high into the air. When they landed, the men marvelled at their uniforms: the elaborate braid on their shoulders, the beautiful, useless helmets, the fine leather of their belts and boots.)

And on and on it went. Hour after hour, day after day, week after week. Stubbs had more or less reached his breaking point. He could stand in a trench up to his thighs in water for hours on end, but could not do anything else. He was certain that, if he was ordered to go over the top, he would refuse. And if someone threatened to shoot him there and then, he would simply stand still and take the bullet.

His moment of truth had happened the day before, when his brigade had been moved forward after a couple of days behind the lines. They were marching along the duckboards when Stubbs realised that the ground beneath his feet was too soft. He looked down. Where he was marching, the duckboards had been blown up and, in their place, someone had lain a row of dead German soldiers, like closely packed railway sleepers. When you walked on them, stuff bubbled up from their mouths—or out of their necks, if they had no head.

None of the horrors he had seen before had particularly bothered him, but for some reason this did.

Deep down, he supposed, he must have some respect for his fellow man. Deep down, he must have hoped that when he died, his body would be treated with some respect. Now he saw that he would be treated . . . well, as badly as he had treated his fellow man when he was alive.

The attack could be only minutes away. Already the troops would be gathering in the trenches. Men would be touching lucky mascots, smoking a last cigarette, checking that the standard issue Bible was stuck firmly in a pocket over their hearts.

The bombardment was getting more intense. Stubbs felt a tap on his shoulder. A sergeant he dimly recognised was standing behind him, leading a group of men with trench ladders. The sergeant gestured for Stubbs to stand to one side, and he spread the fingers of his hand twice. Ten minutes to the attack? Stubbs felt sick. Odd how his mouth could go dry in all that wet.

He jerked his thumb at the dug-out behind him and mimed smoking a cigarette. The sergeant nodded.

The dug-out had been abandoned a couple of weeks before, when a German mortar shell had killed all the men in it. It had been the third time that had happened and the men now thought it unlucky. Now, all that was left of it was a sheet of corrugated iron balanced on top of some broken wooden props and a pile of old ammo boxes to sit on. Stubbs sat down next to a roll of telephone wire and a pot of paint for making the signposts that were the only way to get around the maze of trenches.

He tried to think.

In response to the British guns, the German guns started to fire. Shells exploded either side of the trench, showering it with mud. Shrapnel whistled past. Fragments rattled on the thin iron roof. This would go on until the British 'creeping barrage' started. This was a line of exploding shells that moved slowly forward and cleared the ground in front of it. The idea was that, with the shells landing all around them, the German artillery and machine-gunners would have to keep their heads down, and the British troops could advance in some safety. Of course, it never worked like that.

Stubbs felt panic rising.

An enormous explosion shook the ground, blowing the roof of the shelter high into the air. But as it crashed down inches from Stubbs, a desperate idea came to him. He slipped his rifle off his back, and before he could think things through, dug the sharp edge of the bayonet into his forehead and opened up a jagged wound. At first he could just feel a cold dull pain. Then it quickly turned hot as the blood ran from the wound over his forehead and down into his eyes.

He staggered into the trench, one hand clamped to his forehead, the other waving ahead of him.

'Help me, help me. Oh my God, I can't see! I'm blind!'

His hand was torn away from his forehead and he heard a voice calling for first aid. Stubbs felt hands dab at his forehead and clear the blood from his eyes.

'We haven't got time for this, doc. Just slap a bandage on him and he can sit tight. What's the matter, doc?'

Stubbs looked at the soldier the captain was calling doc, and his heart sank. It was the doctor from the Bullring. The game was up.

'I think you'll find he's fit, sir,' the doctor said.

'Really? What makes you think that?'

'Flesh wound, sir, and self-inflicted. Look at his bayonet tip.'

'What?'

If Stubbs had kept his head he

might have got away with it, but he cracked.

'You bastard!' he shouted. 'You evil bastard!'

'I know this man,' the doctor said. 'He was . . . he's a crook and a coward. He waited for a big shell burst, then nicked his forehead with his bayonet to make it look like a shrapnel wound. I'm sure of it, sir.'

The captain's whole manner changed. Now he spoke in a cold, clipped voice. 'Normally, I'd send you back to HQ in irons or shoot you on the spot. But I've got a better idea. I know how to punish you properly. Doc—tie up that man's head. Sergeant, see that white paint? I don't want to lose this worthless piece of scum in the smoke. Take the brush and paint a white C, big as you like, on the back of his tunic. I'm going to be right behind him with a gun. Right, men, into positions. Wait for it. Wait for it. Remember, men— the barrage moves at a steady marching pace. No slacking! Keep up the pace! No one wants to get caught in the open!'

He took out a pocket watch.

The barrage from the British guns started up with a new fury. Faintly, from the left and right, came the sound of whistles. The sergeant blew his, and Stubbs found himself being pushed up the ladder and over the top of the trench. He felt the captain's gun in his back, heard him shouting and then simply concentrated on putting one foot in front of the other.

Ahead of him he could see the flashes of the shells exploding through the wall of smoke. For about five yards, the going was awful. Then it got worse. It was a huge effort just to lift his feet up out of the sucking mud.

Another five yards, and the mud was over his knees. Stubbs found that just lifting his leg high enough to take a step sent burning waves of agony along his thighs. One step, then another, then another.

'On, on!' The captain's voice was high and frantic.

No wonder. The men were making almost no progress and the barrage was moving further and further ahead. By now they should have gone a hundred yards. In fact, they had not moved a hundred feet and the line of men was broken as they all struggled to move forward in any way they could.

He heard the captain shout 'Hold the line! Hold the line!' but it was hopeless. Stubbs decided to make progress as slow as possible, slipping and falling, and then taking an age to get up. Now it was getting really important to find shelter. If the barrage passed over the first few German guns without knocking them out, the British soldiers would be caught in the open. They would be sitting ducks.

The going got even harder. They

were creeping up a slight rise. In front of them the ground was dotted with broken trees. Trunks were blasted off about two feet from the ground. Roots twisted their way through the mud as if they were desperate to escape. The roots tripped them; the trunks forced them to find ways round them. There were bodies everywhere. Bodies and bits of bodies. Stubbs rested his weight on a tree trunk to try and get his breath back. His lungs felt as if they were on fire and he had lost a boot in the mud somewhere.

Then he felt his senses sharpen and he peered ahead. The smoke from the barrage was beginning to thin, and he thought he had seen something grey and solid out there.

'Keep moving, man! Hurry!' The captain jabbed at him.

He took a step. Then another. Directly ahead lay a crater so big that it could only have been made by one of the huge mortar shells. There was a pool of water at the bottom. But because they were on a slight rise, the water table was that much lower and the sides of the crater would give some protection.

'Don't stop or I'll—'

Two things happened at the same time. Twenty yards ahead of them a machine gun started up, flashes flickering through the smoke. At the same time, a shell exploded in the air ten yards behind them. Stubbs and the officer were blown forward by the blast into the crater.

Stubbs felt himself slip down the muddy sides of the hole. He let go of his rifle and dug into the mud with his fingernails.

His feet splashed into the water. It rose higher and higher. Now it was round his knees, now his thighs, now his chest. He'd seen men hide themselves in craters only to drown. He forced his fingers into the mud and, just as he felt the chill wet of the water tickle his chin, he managed to hold on.

The water was helping him to float. By plunging his hands deep into the mud, he managed to work his way round the edge of the pool to where the sides were not so steep. Above him, he could see the officer crawling towards the crater's rim.

He followed.

The German machine gun just in front of them was firing non-stop now, and sounded very close. Stubbs lifted his head very slowly above the crater's edge. The gun was in a concrete pillbox, its muzzle poking out from the dark slit. It was so close that he could see the detail of its barrel. It was familiar to him, of course: the gun the Germans used to mow down the Allies was almost the same gun that the Allies used to mow down the Germans.

The captain climbed sideways until he was close to Stubbs. 'Right, Private,' the captain said, 'no one's going anywhere fast as long as that gun is pinning us down. What say we take it out?'

Stubbs glanced at the officer. This was the same man who had driven him into battle at gunpoint?

'What do you suggest, sir?' he asked.

'Right, what I'm asking you to do isn't going to be easy. In fact, you are going to need a cool head and every scrap of grit you've got. I want you to go about ten feet in that direction over there and take a few shots at the pillbox to draw his fire. That should give me enough time to stick my head up and post a couple of Mills bombs down the letter box. Do this and . . . well, I'll forget the little incident earlier, eh?'

'Got a decent arm on you, have you, sir?' Stubbs asked. 'First eleven were you, sir?'

'As a matter of fact . . .' Something in the blank tone of Stubbs's voice must have got through to him. 'I say, are you taking this seriously?

Because I can assure you, you're in enough trouble as it is.'

'In trouble?' Stubbs said. 'With you?' His voice dripped with contempt. 'We're drowning in mud. There's a machine gun wants to kill us. Bombs are dropping everywhere and you want me to be polite?'

'I want you to show respect. It's a matter of discipline,' the captain said. 'Now, where's your rifle?'

'Lost it, sir. It came off when I was trying not to drown.'

The captain looked at him closely. 'Listen to me, man. I'm going to be frank with you. This is your only chance to wipe the slate clean. I know there's a good man in there, Stubbs. I'm going to trust you. I'm going to give you my Webley pistol. Now it kicks like a mule, but it can stop an elephant. What do you say? Do you think you can repay my trust and be the man I know you can be?'

Stubbs looked into the captain's eyes. 'You're right, sir. This is my chance. Let me prove to you what sort of chap I really am.'

'I knew I could count on you,' the captain said. 'Well done. Are you clear what you've got to do?'

'Yes sir.' The captain handed Stubbs the Webley, crawled to the top of the crater, while Stubbs slid about ten feet away.

'When I shout "Now".'

The officer laid his hand grenades out in front of him, pulled the pin out of one of them and shouted, 'Now!' Stubbs watched him stand, pull his arm back and lob the grenade. When the bomb was in mid-air, Stubbs shot him.

The captain had not been exaggerating. The kick from the pistol almost broke Stubbs's wrist, but the captain was knocked back a good two feet as the blunt lead bullet, almost half an inch across, slammed into him. Half a second later the grenade exploded and the machine gun fell silent. Stubbs waited, then pushed himself up, inch by inch. Black smoke was still drifting from the slit in the pillbox, and the gun's barrel was pointing limply at the ground.

Stubbs took a deep breath. 'Your luck's turned, Johnny boy,' he said to himself. The captain's last act would make his escape that much easier.

But now he had to get busy.

At the bottom of the crater, half in the water, his feet pointing at the sky, was a dead British soldier. With extreme care, Stubbs lowered himself down the side of the crater until he was on a level with the dead man's trouser cuffs. Then he started to haul him up. It seemed to take forever, because it was almost impossible to drag him up without slipping down. In the end, he took off his tunic, tied one sleeve to a tree trunk, looped the other round his wrist and was able to drag the body up the slope one-handed. Then he wedged the dead man's boots into a knot of tree roots to stop him slipping down again.

Now for the hard bit.

The body had no head. Stubbs closed his eyes and started to feel around the neck for his identity tag. Where was it?

His fingers scrabbled more desperately, cutting themselves on the man's broken spine. It was gone! The bastard's ID tag had slipped off.

Stubbs swore loudly. The tag was the first thing he needed if he was going to change identities. Still, all was not wasted. He needed another tunic, one without a sodding great white C painted on it.

His numb fingers started to work at the dead man's buttons.

*   *   *

The sounds of battle had moved away by the time Stubbs had finished. The other guy's tunic was a bit tight across the chest, but then you can't have everything. He looked at the captain and patted his chest. His fingers told him there was a nice fat wallet in there.

Stubbs's heart lifted, and he took this as a sign that Lady Luck was smiling on him again. But just as his fingers closed on the fine leather of the wallet, he felt the captain's hand grip his wrist with horrible, desperate strength.

'So, you're a thief as well.'

His words were distorted. Stubbs thought he had hit him in the chest, but the bullet must have been deflected upwards by something and smashed into his jaw. That's why the bastard wasn't dead. Stubbs tried to wrench his hand away but the wounded officer hung on.

Stubbs had been brought up on the streets, though. He brought his mouth up to the captain's broken jaw, bit down and started to worry it like a dog.

The captain screamed and let go.

Stubbs pulled himself up on top of the officer, put his knees on his shoulders and started to smash his fists into his head.

CHAPTER FIVE

It was pitch black in the cellar, but at last Private Christopher Ransom heard footsteps cross the room above him, and saw light appear in the gaps between the floorboards.

Ever since he had remembered who he was, he had been trying to attract someone's attention. Now he felt his way to the cellar steps, climbed them and started banging on the door with his fists.

Light appeared underneath it and a voice said: 'Stand back from the door or I'll shoot you.'

Ransom backed down the stairs. The door opened a chink, then wider. He saw the shape of the sergeant with a revolver in his hand.

'Bring that light!' he ordered.

Ransom saw the mud on his uniform and his drawn exhausted face. He seemed to be swaying from side to side.

'I'm sorry, Sarge,' he gabbled. 'I've been waiting all day and no one was here. I know who I am. I've remembered.'

The sergeant's eyes seemed to focus for the first time.

'What?' he asked.

'I know who I am. You remember, Sarge. At the trial they said I was John Stubbs or someone, but I'm not. I'm Private Christopher Ransom, Number 3 Section, B Battery, the 4th Artillery Brigade.'

'You know what?' the sergeant said. 'I've just come back from Polygon Wood. They reckon 20,000 men have died there this summer and no one knows what their bloody names are. What makes you so special?'

73

'I know, sir, but—'

'Shut it, Private. If you can find out what happened and prove it, maybe you'll get the court to change its mind, but don't count on it. And don't think anyone's going to do anything about it tonight.'

And he slammed the door.

Ransom sank back onto his metal bed frame. For a minute despair overcame him again. The sergeant was right. With all that killing going on, why would anyone care about a case of mistaken identity—even if it was a matter of life and death. A rat ran across the floor and knocked against his foot. He made as if to kick it, and then stopped himself. No. The rat had as much right to life as he did.

What had happened? What had happened to Chris Ransom to turn him into John Stubbs? He forced his mind to go back in time.

* * *

74

He remembered being back in the stables after he had led his team back from the field guns. He had been badly shaken up by the events of the morning—the noise of the shells, the broken bodies and his own narrow escape—but he found comfort in brushing down the horses. This was not really his job, but the grooms were happy for him to do it. As Ransom brushed the mud from a horse's flanks, he felt as if he were cleaning his mind of the memories. He leaned his head against the great beast's chest, felt its warmth against his cheeks, heard the huge double drumbeat of his heart.

That was how Sergeant Mitchell found him.

'You got back, sir,' Ransom said.

'I got back. I had to shoot four horses: two wounded, two in the mud. I've got some good news for you though. Leave's been granted and I've got your pass.' He held up the sheet of paper. 'Yes, it's real. Better take it. Starts tomorrow—from noon on, you're a free man. Who knows, by the time you get back, the war might be over.' But instead of wheeling smartly and marching out, he stayed, shuffling from foot to foot.

Ransom felt he knew him well enough to ask: 'Everything all right, sir?'

'Not exactly. The water mains have been blown to buggery again and there are lads out there who haven't had a drink all day. Two days for some of them. There's a wagon hitched up to a couple of mules, but no one to drive it. The transport crew's all shot up and their replacements are tied up behind the lines. I'll not beat about the bush. It's unfair, what with leave coming up and all that, but I don't think there's another man in the company who could get our long-eared chums to the front through all this.'

Ransom noticed that he had not been asked in so many words if he would volunteer.

'Mules, Sarge?' If horses were called long-faced chums, mules were long-eared chums and much hated by one and all. Stubborn, stupid and slow, they made their drivers' lives as miserable as possible.

'That's the way it is.'

'That's a cruel twist of fate.'

'For someone.'

'Permission to volunteer, sir.'

'There's no . . . You don't have to . . .' For a second, the sergeant seemed lost for words. Then his spine stiffened. 'Permission granted, Private. Now listen. There's the big tank, and then we've added about fifty canteens of water on top. Get it to the front, unhitch it and come back. It's not your job to give the water out. You're more use here. Understood?'

'Yes, Sarge.'

'And don't be a hero, right?'

77

'Right, Sarge.'

* * *

To be honest, the mules weren't too bad. The lead one was saddled, but Ransom knew that they preferred to be led. Like men, if mules were asked to go somewhere, they wanted proof that the person doing the asking was prepared to make the effort.

For the first quarter-mile or so, the road was well protected by a low bank to the right. After that, it was in full view of the enemy, but with any luck, they'd be fully taken up dealing with the attack that was still going on. A bit of ground had been gained to the north of the bulge, and in the damp, still air ragged drifts of shell smoke wandered the landscape like ghosts.

Rain did not so much fall as drift around, as if it did not want to touch the ground. It gathered on the ears of the mules and on the rim of Ransom's helmet. He passed a long, straggling line of soldiers on their way back to barracks for a rest. Some of them asked for water, but were told to pipe down by their mates. 'Plenty where we're going. You get as far forward as you can, mate. The lads at the front need all the water they can get.'

He trudged on. Shells from British field guns screamed low overhead. Shells from German guns shot back. Ransom put his head down and tramped on.

The next thing he knew, he was off the road, and flat on his back. It felt as if two bricks had clapped him on both ears. He couldn't hear a thing and his brain felt like jelly.

There was a mule moving weakly underneath him, and that was the only thing that stopped him from sinking. The other beast was lying on the duckboard, torn apart by a shell. He rolled over and launched himself across the mud towards the wagon. He just managed to grab hold of a wheel spoke and pull himself up.

His rifle was still in the wagon. He fed a round into the breech, shot the drowning mule, then wondered what to do—until he heard a little voice in his head. *The lads at the front need all the water they can get.*

He loaded himself with canteens, first over one shoulder, then over the other. Then he headed down the road.

*   *   *

He was not sure where he was. Occasionally he came across street signs, crudely painted on scraps of wood: Park Lane, Piccadilly, Hellfire Corner. He came across bodies, some old and some new. He came to a ladder and climbed it, then immediately fell up to his knees in mud. He waded on. Bullets zipped past him, sending splatters of water into his face. Suddenly he realised that the strange, muddy shapes that broke up the surface of the mud were bodies. He went from one to the other. Not one was alive. The canteens weighed him down, making progress even harder. He saw a concrete pillbox in front of him. Its gun was silent. He was looking at it so hard that he almost fell into a large crater.

There he saw the strangest sight. In the crater were two living men, fighting hand to hand in the mud. They were British soldiers.

'Hey!' he shouted. 'Hey! Stop that.'

A bullet whizzed past his ear like a very fast wasp. He slid down into the crater, and began to work his way round towards the two men. By the time he reached them, one was definitely winning. He had climbed onto the other and was slamming his fists into him.

Ransom tapped him on the

shoulder. Bloodshot eyes looked out from a blackened face.

'You don't want to do that, mate,' Ransom said.

The soldier tried to punch him. Ransom dodged easily and knocked the man to one side. The man fell into the mud, slid down into the water and started to try to crawl out. Ransom thought that was the best place for him, for the time being.

He turned the other man over, and cleared the mud from his mouth and nostrils. His mouth seemed to go halfway round his face in a terrible open wound. Ransom poured half a canteen of water onto it to get it clean, then lifted his head as gently as possible. He was concentrating so hard, that he did not notice that the other soldier had crawled out of the water and was now crouching behind him.

Ransom had just got some water into the wounded man's mouth, when the other soldier hit him on the back of the head and a black starburst exploded in his brain.

CHAPTER SIX

Stubbs looked at the soldier he had just hit. He was covered with canteens. Seeing them reminded him just how thirsty he was. He pulled one free, drank deeply and felt life coming back into his limbs.

How did that funny old poem go that he had been forced to learn at school?

But if it comes to slaughter
You will do your work on water,
An' you'll lick the bloomin' boots
of 'im
that's got it.

The poem was all about a faithful water carrier called Gunga Din, who died saving the life of a British soldier somewhere out in the Empire. Stubbs, however, was not the type to do any boot-licking. He sat down with a canteen, drank again, and thought about stealing the young captain's dog tag, but rejected the idea. There was no way he could pass himself off as an officer. Officers were in a sort of club where everyone knew everyone else, and he would be found out really quickly.

That left the other guy. He squatted over his chest and pulled his ID free. Ransom. Private Christopher Ransom. He'd have to remember that.

He started going through his pockets. When he pulled out the leave pass, he thought he was dreaming.

This was his big chance! No, this was more than his big chance! This was a sign! This was where his life started all over again!

With a leave pass, he didn't need to rejoin his old unit—or the other poor bastard's old unit. With the pass in one pocket and the officer's cash in the other, he could go back from the front, back through the lines and straight to a French hotel. He'd seen their hotels while he'd been on the march, seen the soldiers eating outside on small metal tables. He thought of beer, steak, a nice pile of spuds done the French way in little crispy strips. He thought of bottles of wine. Christ, with the money he had he could even afford champagne, a bath, a young lady . . .

Funny how life turned out, he thought. He took another swig of water before emptying the rest onto the head of the water carrier. Then he snapped off his identity chain for good measure.

'You're a better man than I am, Private Ransom,' he said. 'But that doesn't count for anything out here.'

He patted his pockets and looked up.

You couldn't mistake a German

coal-scuttle helmet, and there were four of them on the rim of the crater with real German faces underneath. They were no more than fifteen feet away and they had spotted him. One of them pointed. Stubbs searched around for a weapon. Then he noticed something that made his blood run cold.

Three of the Germans were carrying rifles. The other was holding a long thin pipe with flame dripping out of the end. Two canisters were strapped to his back and made his shape seem lumpy and ugly.

A flame-thrower! After gas, that was every soldier's nightmare. The German flame-thrower units had a death's head patch sewn to their uniforms. It was an act of bravado. If they were captured, they were shot on the spot.

Stubbs saw fire spurt from the flame-thrower, and then go out. It had misfired. He looked for the revolver. It was there, on the other side of the officer. But just as he grabbed the gun, someone tugged on his leg. He looked over his shoulder. The water carrier had come round and he was hanging onto his ankle grimly.

Stubbs tried to stand. The water carrier would not let go and came up with him. Above him, on the rim of the crater, he saw the flames shoot out again and then again.

The German pointed the thrower down the crater as the other soldiers aimed their rifles. They all fired together just as Stubbs, with a huge effort, hauled the water carrier to his feet and forced him round so he formed a living shield. The flames enclosed them. Stubbs felt his hands cook as the burning oil hit them. He screamed and whirled round. A bullet hit him in the leg. Another took him in the chest. Then the flames were all around him and the pain flashed into a bright cloak of horror as his nerve endings fried.

This is so unfair, he thought. So unfair.

And he died.

CHAPTER SEVEN

Ransom felt the flames enclose him, and saw the other man break away. That saved him because the stream of burning oil followed the moving target.

He threw himself sideways, and felt a terrific blow as a bullet glanced off his tin helmet. He staggered, got tangled up in tree roots and tripped. He blacked out for what seemed like the blink of an eye, but, when he came to, for a moment he couldn't remember what had happened.

He seemed to be hanging upside down above a wall of flames. He thought that he had died and gone to hell. Then he reckoned that even the devil could not create the suffering that he was going through.

The devil, he thought, might have plugged up his nose, might have surrounded him with lumps of rotting flesh, but would surely not have shoved the flesh up his nostrils. The devil might have been tempted to burn him, but would surely have dipped him in burning oil. He would not have painted the stuff onto the most faraway parts of his body and set it burning slowly. The devil would not have thought of hanging him upside down over someone's severed head that was bobbing slowly in filthy water. Surely the devil would not have thought to make everything so damn itchy. That was the effect of flames on muddy skin.

No, Ransom thought. This wasn't hell. This was the British Army. This was what he had signed up for. He just had to stick it out.

Then something gave way and he fell into the water.

He slid in so cleanly that his head hit the soft mud at the bottom of the crater and stuck there. The water canisters fell and tangled themselves around his legs and arms. He could not tell what was up and what was down. He just knew that he was drowning. Something bumped into him, but he didn't like to think what it was. Then his legs fell sideways, his head came unstuck from the mud, and he forced himself to thrash around a bit more. His face broke the surface of the water.

He took a few breaths and struggled to the edge of the water. He kicked hard to stop himself from sinking, but felt the weight of his clothes dragging him down.

He heard a sound coming from above and looked up. Dangling above his head was the sleeve of an army tunic. He wrapped it round his arm. Using it as a support, he reached up and found he could grab one of the tree roots. He managed to pull half the water canteens over his head, swapped hands and worked the others off. Then he levered himself up and crawled to safety. The officer with the shot-up face was lying on his back, staring up at the sky. Ransom fell down next to him. He started to shiver and realised how cold he was.

It wasn't that surprising: the clothes had been burned off his back, but the thick mud, wetness and the water canteens that he had been carrying had protected him from the worst of the flames.

What could he wear? He reached down, untied the tunic from the tree root and put it on. Moving about made him feel better.

He crawled back to the officer, who grabbed him and tried to say something. Ransom saw his tongue working through a hole in his cheek and bent his head closer to the man.

'What?' he asked.

'See,' the officer seemed to be

saying. He lifted a hand and pointed to Ransom's new tunic.

Deep down in Ransom's mind was a memory of the man he had seen going through his own tunic pockets. That must be what the officer was trying to tell him. The soldier had stolen something from him.

Suddenly he remembered and the memory was like a shaft of warm sunlight. He had been going on leave! He had been given his papers! He was going to get out of this terrible place.

He patted the officer.

'Thank you, sir,' he said. 'Thank you. It's getting dark. I'm going to get you out of here now. We're going back. We'll be all right soon. Right as rain.'

Then he thought that was probably the wrong phrase. He would never think there was anything right about rain ever again.

*   *   *

It took Ransom six hours to get the captain back to the lines. It was impossible to be certain which direction they were heading in. He just aimed for the gun flashes on the horizon and hoped they were Allied guns.

When he found a row of sandbags, he knew they had made it. He dragged the officer up to the sandbank wall and pushed him to the top. They both fell over together, waking a sentry.

After that, everything was very confusing. The officer was taken off on a stretcher, while Ransom was made to sit on a pile of sandbags and be questioned by a sergeant. Everyone seemed to be making a huge fuss of him, but did not know who he was. They found some leave papers, but they also found someone else's name tag stuffed into a pocket. That created problems.

Then someone said: 'He's got

something painted on the back of his tunic. Looks like the letter C.'

And someone else said: 'Captain Bradshaw did that to some bastard who was trying to get out of the attack.'

'Bradshaw must have brought him all the way back. What's his name?'

'I don't know. Stubbs or something.'

'That's it. The identity tag says he's Private John Stubbs. He must have nicked some other poor bastard's leave papers.'

'All right, all right,' the sergeant said. 'We'll get him back to HQ. If half of this is true, it'll be a court martial for him.'

CHAPTER EIGHT

As the memories flooded his mind, Ransom felt a huge weight lift. Dawn was breaking. From the light that crept in through the airbrick, he could see that it was going to be a fine day.

Now that he could explain what had happened, he was sure to be released. They'd tried the wrong man. The real Private Stubbs was lying dead in the crater by the pillbox. They could find him. Then they could find Sergeant Mitchell.

Not a minute could be wasted. So he started pounding on the door again.

*   *   *

Half an hour later, the sergeant major went to the officers' mess. It was the same room in which the court martial had been held, but now it was much warmer. The big windows were open and scents from the overgrown garden outside blew in.

The officers were eating pork chops, fried eggs, fried potatoes, fried tomatoes and fried mushrooms. The sergeant major made a mental note to head off to the kitchens, after he had done this tricky job, and eat up the remains. It was a privilege of his rank. And a good breakfast, he always believed, helped keep body and soul together.

After he had stood to attention for about a minute, one of the officers found time to look up at him.

'Wallflowers, Sergeant, don't you think? Or stock?'

'Sir?'

'The scent coming in through the door. Haven't you got any poetry in your soul, man?'

'Wallflowers, sir. I spotted a few coming out yesterday.'

'Bit late, aren't they?'

'Self-seeded, sir. Not forced. And what with the rain and that.'

'Are you a keen gardener, Sergeant?'

'My father runs a nursery, sir, out Enfield way.'

'Your father runs a nursery. Your father runs a nursery.'

The officer spoke the words in mock surprise, making the sergeant feel like a fool for giving him too much information. He wondered if he would ever understand the upper classes. Just when you thought they were human, they went and proved the opposite.

'Well, what is it?' the major barked out the question.

'The prisoner requests the right to see the padre, sir,' the sergeant said. 'He claims it's urgent, sir.'

'When's the execution?' the major asked the table.

'Tomorrow. Dawn. Someone will have to be up for it, I suppose.'

'Quite.' The major turned his attention back to the sergeant. 'Urgent, eh?'

'Yessir.'

'Well, I suppose if he says it's urgent, it is. Who's padre?' he asked the table.

'You know, Ratface Ratcliffe. Good man.'

'Prisoner's in for a shock. Does he still think he's someone else?'

'Seems quite certain, sir,' the sergeant said.

'Is he mad?' The first officer screwed an index finger into his temple.

'Seems to be getting saner, if anything,' the sergeant said.

'Then he really needs shooting,' the major said. 'Ratface will sort it out. Count on it. Good man.'

*　　　*　　　*

Ransom looked at the padre and his heart sank.

The padre would clearly have been happier to interview Ransom from the other side of a desk. Without a desk, he made Ransom sit on the bed, and stood as far away from him as possible. Then he stared at the wall about five feet above his head.

'I think I've worked it all out,' said Ransom. 'When the tunic was burnt off my back by the flame-thrower, I had to look around for a new one. It was tied to a tree root and I just put it on. It must have been Stubbs's. There was a body in the crater without a tunic. Stubbs must have stolen it and left his own lying on the ground. The officer tried to warn me. I understand that now. He pointed at the tunic. He must have been warning me about the C on the back. When I got to our lines, that's what the lads saw. That's what made them think I was Stubbs. Stubbs had stolen the leave papers from me and I got them back off him. It was terrible, sir. He was on fire, but the uniform was so wet, it stopped them burning. Do you see how it could happen, sir?'

The padre rocked on his feet.

'All I see is a load of old rubbish,' he said. 'I never heard so much nonsense in my life. Listen for your own good, now. The truth is seldom complicated. Lies, in my opinion, usually are. The devil spins a web of lies. The good Lord cuts straight through all the rubbish. My advice? Drop all this nonsense. It's cowardly and unmanly, and it's what got you into trouble in the first place. Get some backbone, man. I can't pretend to tell you what the good Lord thinks about you, but I can tell you this: if you admit what you've done, you're in with a fighting chance.'

'But I can't admit something I haven't done,' Ransom said. 'Don't you see? You say admitting my guilt is the only way for me to be saved, but suppose I'm not guilty?'

'Oh, you're guilty, my man,' the padre said. 'Now it's just a question of seeing how you deal with it.'

*   *   *

The padre had been invited to lunch a few miles away, in a pleasant country house. It was far away from the lines, and there were rows of vines in the rolling fields at the back.

The talk over lunch was of morale. Normally it was bad form to talk about the war over a meal but things, apparently, were going from bad to worse.

'It's all very well to say we're helping out the French, but I'm afraid that isn't much comfort when you're up to your neck in mud twelve hours a day,' one man said.

'You're exaggerating,' another said. 'We just have to make sure we don't slack off. It's natural after three years of fighting to want a bit of a break, but that's when the Hun is at his most deadly. He'll sense weakness and strike. That's why we need to keep on attacking. If we get somewhere, good show. If not, it shows the enemy, and the men, that we still mean business. Standing around in all this mud—that is what saps their strength. It gives them time to brood.'

The padre gave a loud bark that got everyone's attention. 'That's exactly right. The stories the men come up with to try and get off the hook!'

'Come on, Ratface, what have you heard?'

'I was in to see a fellow this morning. I have never, ever come across a worse case of pure evil in my time as padre. This little private soldier injured himself to try and get out of the last big push, was caught, and had to be prodded into action at gunpoint. He must have got away, and killed another private to steal his leave papers. Then the officer who caught him in the first place, found him, arrested him and led this wretched little oik all the way back to the lines—even though he's got half his face blown off.'

'Sorry to butt in, sir, but who had their face blown off? The criminal or the officer?' A serious-looking captain at the far end of the table had spoken. He was leaning forward and his brow was wrinkled with concentration.

'What?' the padre said, annoyed by the interruption. 'The officer. But that's not the point. Since then, instead of trying to make peace with his maker, this coward's made up a story that's like one of those Shakespeare plays. People were getting dressed up in the wrong tunic and being mistaken for someone else. If you believe him, he saved the officer's life and more or less carried him back to the lines. I ask you. It gives cowards a bad name, what?'

'Amazing story,' the serious-looking captain said. 'The thing is, Padre, it does rather fit in with a story I heard.'

'What? You mean someone else helped him make up this nonsense?'

'No. It's more serious than that. I suppose this man you saw is going to be tried?'

'Oh, he's been tried and found guilty. He'll be shot tomorrow. Didn't I say?'

'It's just that . . . I heard that an old friend of mine, Bertie Stokes, had been shot up pretty badly, so I tracked him down at the field hospital. He's in a frightful state. Half his face was shot off, and he claims he was attacked by a man he was trying to arrest, and then he was saved by another private. A real hero, this private, by all accounts. He dragged Stokes back across no-man's-land. He'd be dead otherwise. Anyway, it took him most of a morning to tell me this. He was woozy with the morphine the medics had given him, but I could tell he really wanted to tell me. Just before he passed out he said: "Shake his hand for me, will you, and tell the silly sod he put on the wrong tunic." '

The padre looked startled and said: 'This is a joke, isn't it?'

'Absolutely not. Go and see Bertie.

He's in the field hospital right now, but you better be quick. They're short of beds and are moving them into casualty clearing station as quickly as they can.'

*   *   *

The padre was a simple man. When he had gone in to visit the man in the cellar, he was sure he was guilty, because the British Army said he was guilty. Now he was not sure, so he saw it as his clear duty to talk to the wounded officer, Captain Bertram Stokes.

He reached the field hospital by mid-afternoon, but there had been an attack on a place called Glencorse Wood. It had not gone well and it was impossible to talk to anyone.

At last, the padre found a nurse on a break. She was leaning against a water tank, smoking.

'I say,' the padre said, nodding at the cigarette. 'I don't know about that.'

He regretted it straight away. The eyes that turned towards him were a hundred years older than the nurse. She blinked slowly, and looked away into nothing.

'I'm looking for a man. He was in here quite recently. Captain Stokes was his name. Shot up in the face,' he added.

'A lot of men come through here and a lot of them are shot in the face. I don't know the name of a single one of them,' the nurse said. 'But if he came in a few days back, he'd have been moved back to the casualty clearing station.' She pointed away from the front. 'It's that way.'

*   *   *

It was dusk by the time the padre reached the clearing station. It was in a small Belgian town far away from the fighting and shelling.

Compared to the field hospital, the casualty clearing station was calm and organised. It was located in a very old warehouse. The main storage area was being used as the ward, with the offices serving as operating theatres.

The nurse seemed to take an age to go through the records. The padre thought it would have been quicker to have checked every bed. When they did track down Captain Stokes, they found that he was being operated on.

'That means a wait,' the nurse said. 'They make sure they're unconscious before they operate, of course, and some of them take hours to come round again.'

The padre was hungry, but he took a seat by the empty bed in the huge hall and settled down. Then he had an idea. He found another nurse and asked if there was a telephone in the building. He had a very important message for his headquarters.

He was shown to a telephone. After a few minutes the operator connected him.

'I say, this is—' he began.

Then the line went dead.

CHAPTER NINE

Ransom had been given a lantern, a meal and a Bible. He sat in a pool of light, trying to read the words, but finding no comfort. It was all so wrong and he felt so helpless.

His hopes rose as he heard the scrape of the bolts sliding back and saw the big shape of the sergeant major against the light.

'Any news, Sergeant?' he asked.

'No news. All telephone lines are cut. A mortar landed near the telephone exchange. We've taken back Glencorse Wood, which is odd because we were meant to have taken it a week ago. Still, don't suppose you want to know that. Can I do anything for you?'

'No thanks, sir.'

'Just remember, son. We all have to die. It's the way we choose to do it that makes the difference.'

'With all due respect, sir, that's bollocks.'

'Probably is. Well, good night.'

As the sergeant closed the door, he thought that the man—Stubbs or Ransom—was right. The only way to die was to be certain you weren't going to. Then you'd die ignorant but happy.

He glanced up at the sky. It was cloudy. Dawn would come late.

*   *   *

Ransom could not believe that he had slept. One moment he had been staring up at the airbrick, looking for the first, slight hint of light. The next, the door was opening and half a dozen soldiers were tramping down

109

the cellar stairs.

Breakfast was French bread and English tea. The bread was like glue in his mouth; the tea like hot iron filings. He put them both to one side.

'Sorry,' he said. 'Can't eat a thing.'

Feet shuffled.

'Is the padre here?' Ransom asked.

'No. Sorry. Word is, he didn't come back last night.'

'Right. I just thought . . .' Ransom realised that he had been hanging on to a slim thread of hope. Somewhere deep down, he thought that what he had said to the padre might have made a difference.

'Do you want . . .? There's a chaplain. He's French.'

Ransom shook his head. 'What's the point?' he said.

He could barely get the words out. His throat felt as thin as a straw. He couldn't stop thinking of home and suddenly he just wanted it over so the dreadful pain he was feeling

110

would go away.

CHAPTER TEN

The padre had a problem. His watch said three o'clock in the morning, and dawn could not be far off. He had been told that he could not wake the patient under any circumstances, but he knew that, if he didn't, all hope of getting to the truth would be lost.

He watched the patient's eyelids like a hawk and when he saw them flutter, he took him by the arm.

The eyes opened slowly. The patient made a noise that sounded like 'Where am I?' He had bandages around his shoulder and bandages around his jaw.

'In hospital. They've just operated on you.'

The patient's eyes slid round and took in the dog collar. 'Don't worry,' the padre said. 'I'm not here to help you towards a better place. You might say I'm here on a mission of mercy. Water? You want water?'

The man drank greedily.

'You're Captain Stokes?'

'Yes.' He could talk. That was something.

'I've got a rather odd question for you,' the padre said. 'It's a matter of life and death.'

CHAPTER ELEVEN

The sky was heavy with dark clouds and full of rain as they led the prisoner out of the cellar. Even that gloomy light made him blink. He looked up and down the corridor, as if help might magically arrive. The corridor stayed empty.

He was marched out of the front door, then round the back to a village of deserted farm buildings.

They marched him down a cobbled street of empty stables, and into a farmyard with a long black wall running down one side.

The sergeant tied Ransom's hands behind his back and then fixed them to a metal hoop in the wall.

The major who had led the court martial walked down the street, pulling on his gloves. He had shaved and his heavy face glowed in the dull dawn. The firing squad of eight men moved from foot to foot.

'Ready, Sergeant Major?'

'Ready, sir.'

'And one of the rifles is loaded with a blank?'

'That's right, sir.'

'And no one knows who's got it? Good. Time to hood the prisoner.'

The last thing that Ransom saw before the hood went on was an ambulance passing by at the head of the little street. He wondered if it was for him. He heard the sergeant call out 'Ready', but his mind was racing. He thought, wildly, that maybe, just maybe, they had found the injured captain and had brought him all the way to the headquarters to save his life. That was it. He was going to be saved.

He could finally take the leave that was owed him and go back home. He imagined relaxing in the carriage as the train from Paddington rushed towards Exeter. He'd be impatient as the little local train went slowly along the slopes of Dartmoor until it reached his village. But he'd enjoy every tree and field and blade of grass he passed. His father would be waiting at the station with the horse and trap. His mother would be waiting at the old farmhouse door. He could picture the dogs playing round his feet. He could smell his favourite meal cooking. Everything was going to be—

*   *   *

The firing squad was well trained. After the first command they followed the sergeant's hand movements, so the prisoner would not know when the fatal shots were coming. And, because bullets travel faster than sound, Ransom didn't hear the shots from the firing squad and he didn't feel them smash into his chest.

For the padre in the ambulance and the wounded officer lying on a stretcher in the back, the sound of the shots was shocking and obscene. They knew it could mean only one thing.

Hearing horses' hooves on cobbles, the major turned round and was amazed to see an ambulance rushing towards him. He went up to the driver.

'Who the devil's this for?' he asked.

'Officer in the back, sir. Mission of mercy, as it were.'

The major walked round to find

the padre helping a heavily bandaged man down the flimsy wooden steps.

'This is Captain Stokes, sir,' the padre said. 'He might have a story to tell about the . . . prisoner.'

'Just let me see him,' the wounded officer said.

The sergeant major had cut him down and he lay, half on his side, slightly curled up.

'Take his hood off, Sergeant,' the padre said. 'If you wouldn't mind.'

The padre didn't look at the dead man on the ground. He watched the face of the wounded officer. When the hood came off the officer flinched as if he had been struck. Then he composed his face and said: 'That's him. That's the man who saved me. Poor fellow deserved a medal, not a firing squad.'

The padre stood back and took a deep breath. What could he say?

'You tried to do the right thing by coming here.'

'I know. This is a dreadful

injustice. There must be an inquiry. But, whatever else, I will tell his family of his bravery, and I'll make sure he's not forgotten.'

POSTSCRIPT

I hope that no one reading this is trying to find a message. Messages are everywhere in the modern world and we probably think too much of them.

This account was written by me, Captain Bertram Stokes, after the war was over. It was a long time before I could bear to think about it and even longer before I could bring myself to put pen to paper. The whole bloody war was like that scene in the crater. Good men killing bad men. Bad men killing good men. Cowardice and courage. Selfishness and sacrifice. But war is like a big machine that devours everything with equal relish: the good and the bad, the weak and the strong. It's only the lucky that get out.

For years I struggled to set the record straight but I failed. I should never have said that Ransom was a hero. If officials refuse to admit that these kangaroo courts martial were wrong to sentence poor shell-shocked boys to death, they'll never admit that they shot a hero by mistake.

No, once a man is dead, that is that. The events are carved into the record as clearly as those hundreds of thousands of names are chiselled into stone memorials from Flanders to small villages all over these islands. Perhaps one day, someone will see this story and help set the record straight. One good turn deserves another but sometimes the debt is so great it can never be repaid. Only remembered.